A JUST ONE MORE BOOK
Just For You

# The Penguins Paint

by Valerie Tripp

Illustrated by Sandra Cox Kalthoff

Developed by The Hampton-Brown Company, Inc.

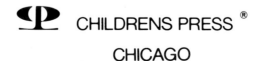
CHILDRENS PRESS ®

CHICAGO

## Word List

Give children books they can read by themselves, and they'll always ask for JUST ONE MORE. This book is written with 82 of the most basic words in our language, all repeated in an appealing rhythm and rhyme.

| | | | |
|---|---|---|---|
| a | get | new | that |
| all | grandma | night | the |
| and | grass | nose | them |
| are | green | | then |
| as | | on | they |
| at | hay | one | to |
| | he | | too |
| best | | paint(ed) | tree |
| black | I | passing | |
| blue | in | penguin(s) | uncle |
| blows | is | Penny | |
| bought | | | wall |
| but | just | rainbow | walk |
| by | | red | wanted |
| | know | | was |
| color(s) | | said | we |
| corn | leaves | sea | went |
| | let's | she | whales |
| day | like(d) | sky | what |
| do | | snow | which |
| don't | many | so | white |
| | more | spring | wind |
| fall | Mrs. | store | world |
| fine | | sun | |
| fish | | swims | yellow |
| fox | | | |

**Library of Congress Cataloging-in-Publication Data**

Tripp, Valerie, 1951-
  The Penguins paint.

  Summary: The Penguins tire of their black and white world and decide to make things more colorful.
  [1.  Penguins — Fiction.  2.  Color — Fiction.
3.  Stories in rhyme]  I.  Kalthoff, Sandra Cox, ill.
PZ8.3.T698Pe  1987     [E]      87-14081
ISBN 0-516-01567-2

2 3 4 5 6 7 8 9 10 11 R 02 01 00 99 98 97 96 95 94

The Penguins' world
was black and white,
white as snow,
black as night.

But all the Penguins
wanted more.
So they went on a walk
to the new paint store.

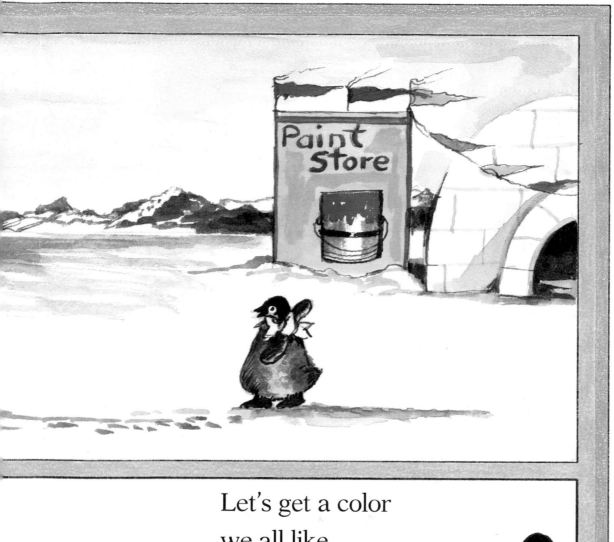

Let's get a color
we all like
and color all
the black and white!

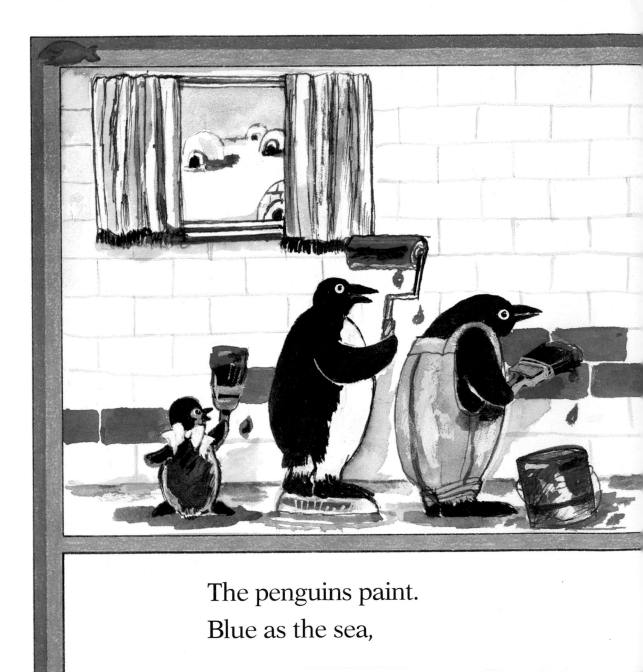

The penguins paint.
Blue as the sea,

Blue as the sky,
Blue as the whales passing by.

But Uncle Penguin
wanted more.

So he bought GREEN
at the new paint store.

The penguins paint.
Green as the grass,

Green as a tree,
Green as a fish that swims in the sea.

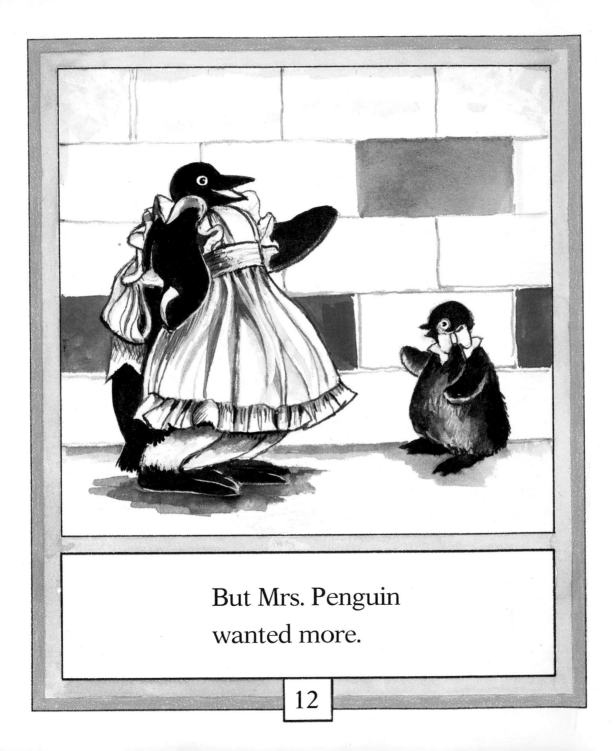

But Mrs. Penguin
wanted more.

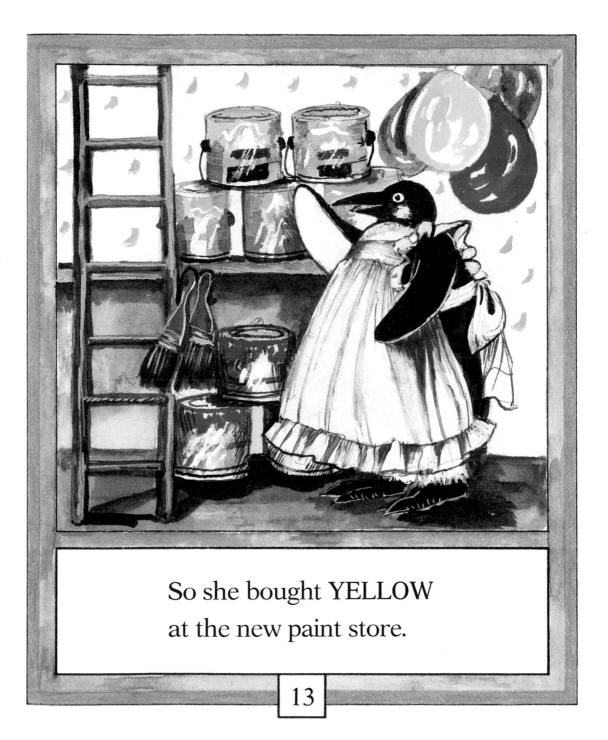

So she bought YELLOW
at the new paint store.

The penguins paint.
Yellow as corn,

Yellow as hay,
Yellow as sun on a fine spring day.

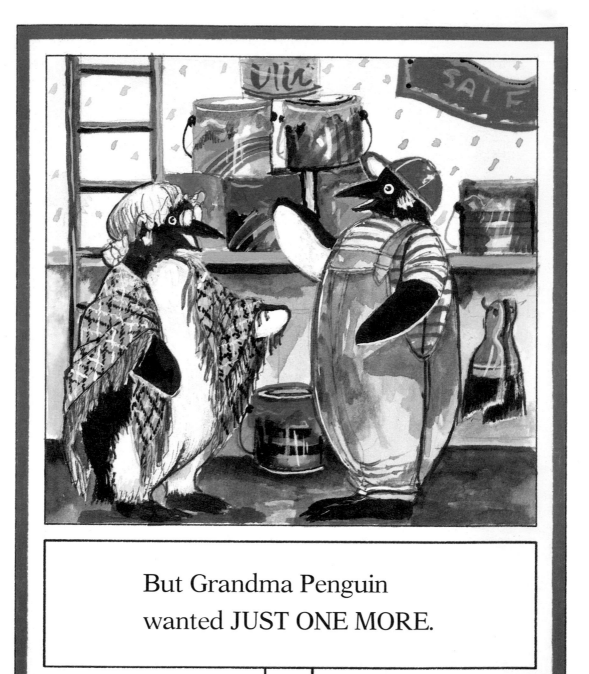

But Grandma Penguin
wanted JUST ONE MORE.

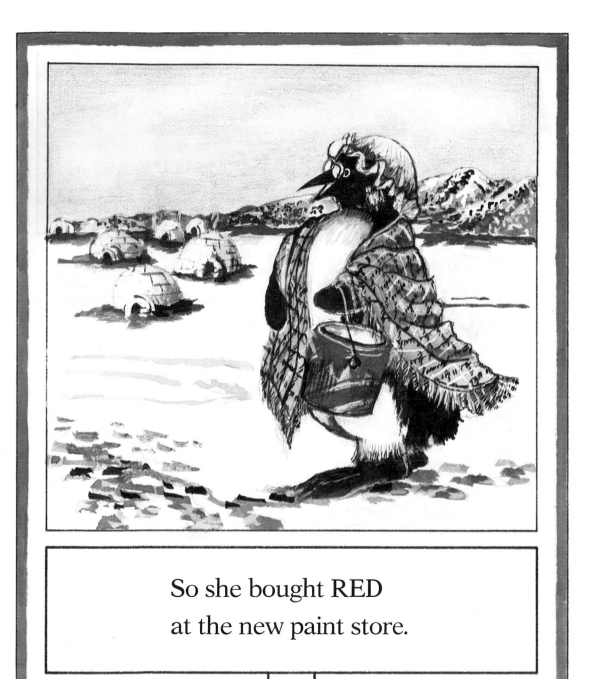

So she bought RED
at the new paint store.

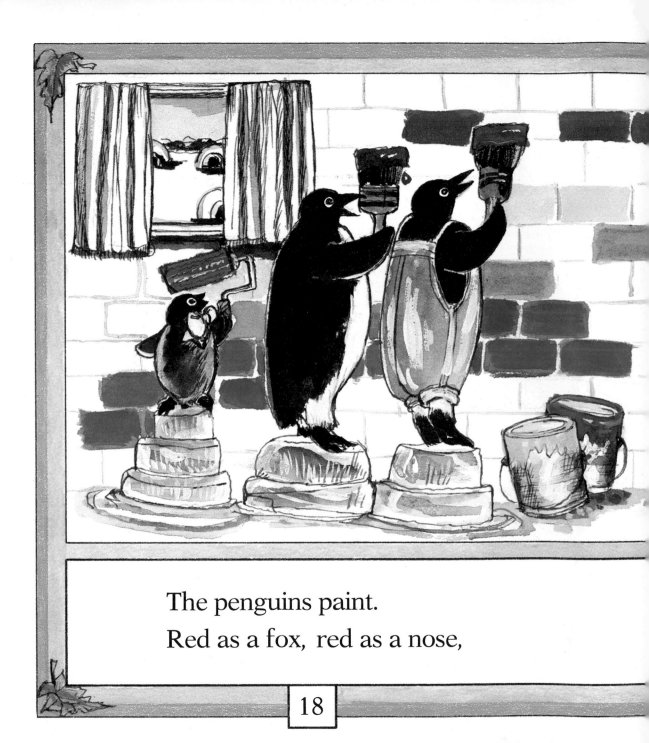

The penguins paint.

Red as a fox, red as a nose,

Red as the leaves
a fall wind blows.

So many colors
are on the wall.
Which one is best?
We like them all.

We like the green.
We like red, too.
We like yellow,
and we all like blue.

21

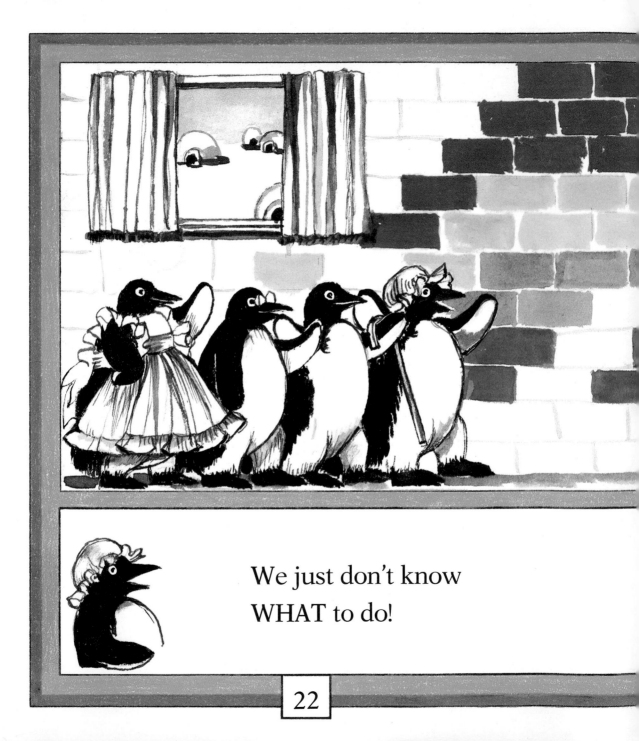

We just don't know
WHAT to do!

Then Penny Penguin said:

I KNOW!

We liked them ALL

and painted....

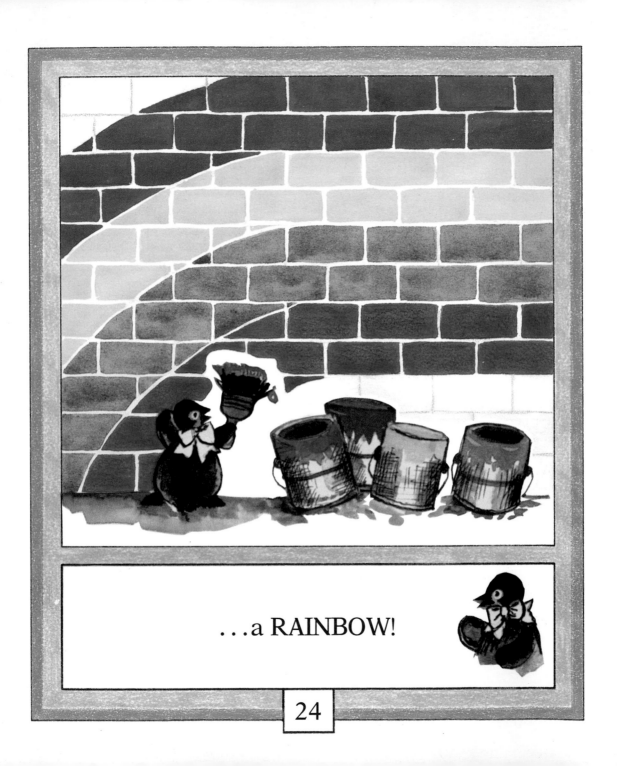

...a RAINBOW!